POKéMON

All Things Bright and Beautifly

Adapted by
Tracey West and
Katherine Noll

SCHOLASTIC INC.
New York Toronto London Auckland Sydney
Mexico City New Delhi Hong Kong Buenos Aires

Published by Scholastic Inc.
90 Old Sherman Turnpike, Danbury, CT 06816.

SCHOLASTIC and associated logos are trademarks and/or registered trademarks of
Scholastic Inc.

ISBN 0-439-72190-3

First Scholastic Printing, May 2005

"Look," said Max one sunny day. "There is Rustboro City."

"Yay!" said Ash. "I am ready for my Gym battle!"

But before they could get to the Gym, Ash saw something strange.

"What are those Trainers doing with their Pokémon?" he asked.

"They are getting ready for a Pokémon Contest," Max said.

"What is that?" Ash asked.

**Before Max could explain, a
Pokémon flew at them. It landed
on May's head!**

"Oh no!" May screamed.

"I wonder what it is?" Ash said. He checked his Pokédex.

"Beautifly, the Butterfly Pokémon," said his Pokédex. "Beautifly have long, thin noses that they use to drink the pollen out of flowers."

A girl and boy ran up.

"Sorry," said the girl. "My name is Janet. That is my Beautifly."

"And my name is Chaz," said the boy. He had a Venomoth on his shoulder. "We are training our Pokémon for the Contest today."

11

"What happens at a Pokémon Contest?" Ash asked.

"In a Contest, Pokémon are judged by how beautiful their attacks are," Janet explained. "Judges give points for every attack."

"That sounds cool," May said. "I want to enter the Contest."

"I want to enter, too," Brock added.

"Let's *all* enter the Contest!" Ash cried.

But there was only one space left in the Contest. And Jessie from Team Rocket got it!

"If I win this Contest," thought Jessie, "I will be a star!"

"You can still watch the Contest," Janet said. "And Max and May can be my assistants."

"Yay!" cried Max and May.

While they waited for the Contest to start, Ash talked to Chaz.

"I cannot wait to battle at the Rustboro City Gym," Ash said.

"But that is a Rock Gym," Chaz pointed out. "Pikachu is an Electric Pokémon. It will have a hard time beating the Rock Pokémon there."

"I can teach you an attack that will help," added Chaz.

He threw a Poké Ball. Sentret came out. "Sentret, use Iron Tail to smash that rock!" Chaz said.

Sentret jumped up. Its tail glowed. Then it smashed a big rock to bits!

"Pika!" cheered Pikachu.

"You will need a strong tail to do Iron Tail," Chaz told Pikachu.

Ash and Pikachu started training right away. Pikachu lifted rocks with its tail to make its tail stronger.

While Ash and Pikachu trained, the Pokémon Contest started.

Max, May, Brock, and Janet stood offstage and watched.

POKÉMON CONTEST

Chaz and his Venomoth were first to go.

Venomoth did Confusion Control. It made things float in the air around it. The judges gave Venomoth a high score!

Outside, Ash and Pikachu kept training. Ash threw balls at Pikachu's tail. Pikachu batted them away.

Then Ash remembered.
"Hey!" he said. "We are missing the Contest!"

They got to the stadium just in time to see Janet and Beautifly using Hidden Power.

Beautifly flew high. Light beams sparkled down on the crowd. It was beautiful.

The judges loved it. Beautifly got a perfect score!

22

Then a strange contestant came out onstage.

It was Jessie in disguise. Meowth and James were disguised as her assistants.

Jessie asked her Seviper to do lots of attacks. But Seviper did not know any of them.

"Boo!" yelled the crowd.

"Seviper, try Poison Tail!" Jessie finally cried.

Seviper did Poison Tail—on *Jessie*! It did not get any points.

Then it was time for the finals.
"The two top Trainers are Chaz
and Janet!" Max said. "They will
have a special battle with Venomoth
and Beautifly."

The battle began.

Venomoth used Stun Spore. It blasted Beautifly with orange poison particles.

Beautifly used Gust. It blew away Venomoth's Stun Spore!

"Beautifly, use Hidden Power!"
Janet cried.

"Venomoth, dodge it!" Chaz yelled.
But Venomoth could not dodge
the Hidden Power attack. It got zapped
by Beautifly's sparkling light beams.

Venomoth fought back. It hit Beautifly with Psybeam.

Rainbow beams shot from Venomoth's eyes. They hit Beautifly. Beautifly fell from the air!

Beautifly recovered. It used Morning Sun. Soft light glowed all over its body.

Beautifly hit Venomoth with Hidden Power again. Then time ran out! Janet had more points!

"Janet wins!" said the judges.

29

Jessie, James, and Meowth ran onstage. They were still wearing disguises.

"Here are some special flowers for you," James told Janet.

But the flowers were a trick. They burst into smoke! No one could see!

Team Rocket captured Beautifly
and Venomoth in nets. Then they took
off their disguises.

"If I cannot win the Contest,
I will steal the winning Pokémon!"
Jessie cried. "Seviper, go!"

31

Ash called on Pikachu. "Use Iron Tail on Seviper!" he yelled.

Pikachu tried to use Iron Tail. Its tail glowed white—for just a second. But it did not work.

"Torchic, help us out!" May cried.

The little Fire Pokémon popped
out of its Poké Ball.

Wham! Torchic used Peck to slam into Seviper. Then it used Ember to burn through the nets holding Beautifly and Venomoth. The two Bug Pokémon flew free.

"Go, Double Gust!" Janet and Chaz yelled.

Beautifly and Venomoth flapped their wings. They made a powerful wind that blew Team Rocket away.

The judges gave Janet a Rustboro Ribbon.

"It is beautiful!" May said. "I want to win one some day."

"You will have to keep training," Max said.

"I will," May said.

"Pikachu and I will keep training, too," Ash said.

"Pika! Pika!" Pikachu said.

Pokémon TRIVIA

Who's That Bug Pokémon?

37

See page 45 or your *Bug Pokédex* for the answer.

Bugging Out

How well do you know your Bug Pokémon? Answer each question to find out if you are a Bug Pokémon Master!

 Which of these Bug Pokémon is also a Fighting Type?

Scizor™   Heracross™

 Which of these Bug Pokémon is also a Steel Type?

Cascoon™   Forretress™

38

3. ## Which of these Bug Pokémon is also a Flying Type?

Beautifly™

Dustox™

 4. ## Which of these Bug Pokémon is also a Poison Type?

Caterpie™

Weedle™

 5. ## Which of these Bug Pokémon is also a Grass Type?

Paras™

Ledyba™

39

Check page 45 or your
Bug Pokédex for the answers.

Battle Time!

Now it is your turn to battle! Read about each battle below. Then pick the best Pokémon to use against your opponent. In each battle, all of the Pokémon are the same level.

1. Uh-oh! Your opponent's Pinsir sure looks scary! Which of these Pokémon can stand up to this Bug Pokémon?

Charmeleon™
(Fire)

Sunflora™
(Grass)

Poochyena™
(Dark)

2. Look! It's a wild Grass Pokémon, Cacnea. Which of these Pokémon will last the longest against it?

Trapinch™
(Ground)

Squirtle™
(Water)

Pineco™
(Bug)

3. Luvdisc may look sweet. But you will need to choose a Pokémon that has the best chance to beat this Water Pokémon. Which will you choose?

Slugma™
(Fire)

Bagon™
(Dragon)

Nosepass™
(Rock)

41

Check page 45 or your *Pokédex* books for the answers.

Attack of the Bug Pokémon!

Different Pokémon have different moves.
Answer the questions to see how well you
know these Bug Pokémon attacks.

1. Which Pokémon can tangle you up
in its Spider Web attack?

Ariados™   Yanma™   Parasect™

2. Which Pokémon can send you flying
with its Gust attack?

Pinsir™   Anorith™   Beautifly™

42

3. Which Pokémon uses Harden to defend itself?

Shuckle™   Surskit™   Metapod™

4. Ouch! Name the Pokémon with Poison Sting.

Ledian™   Weedle™   Pineco™

5. Which Pokémon uses a sharp Slash attach?

Scyther™   Volbeat™   Cascoon™

43

Check page 45 or your *Bug Pokédex* for the answers.

Bug Pokémon Jokes

What did Misty say to the Caterpie?

Quit bugging me!

What is Venomoth's favorite school subject?

Moth-ematics!

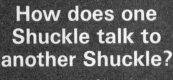

How does one Shuckle talk to another Shuckle?

They use shell-phones!

What happened when two Spinarak fell in love?

They had a webbing!

How does Beedrill get to school?

It takes the school buzz!

How do Volbeat start a race?

Ready, set, glow!

Answers

Page 37: Who's That Bug Pokémon?
Wurmple!

Pages 38–39: Bugging Out
1. Heracross
2. Forretress
3. Beautifly
4. Weedle
5. Paras

Pages 40–41: Battle Time!
1. Charmeleon (Fire beats Bug)
2. Pineco (Bug beats Grass)
3. Bagon (Dragon beats Water)

Pages 42–43: Attack of the Bug Pokémon!
1. Ariados
2. Beautifly
3. Metapod
4. Weedle
5. Scyther